Dear Parent:
Your child's love of reading starts here!

Every child learns to read in a different way and at his or her own speed. You can help your young reader improve and become more confident by encouraging his or her own interests and abilities. You can also guide your child's spiritual development by reading stories with biblical values and Bible stories, like I Can Read! books published by Zonderkidz. From books your child reads with you to the first books he or she reads alone, there are I Can Read! books for every stage of reading:

SHARED READING
Basic language, word repetition, and whimsical illustrations, ideal for sharing with your emergent reader.

BEGINNING READING
Short sentences, familiar words, and simple concepts for children eager to read on their own.

READING WITH HELP
Engaging stories, longer sentences, and language play for developing readers.

READING ALONE
Complex plots, challenging vocabulary, and high-interest topics for the independent reader.

ADVANCED READING
Short paragraphs, chapters, and exciting themes for the perfect bridge to chapter books.

I Can Read! books have introduced children to the joy of reading since 1957. Featuring award-winning authors and illustrators and a fabulous cast of beloved characters, I Can Read! books set the standard for beginning readers.

A lifetime of discovery begins with the magical words **"I Can Read!"**

Visit www.icanread.com for information on enriching your child's reading experience.
Visit www.zonderkidz.com for more Zonderkidz I Can Read! titles.

Shout to the Lord with joy, everyone on earth.
—*Psalm 100:1*

Jesus Loves Me
Copyright © 2008 by Zondervan
Illustrations copyright © 2008 by Hector Borlasca
Adapted from Stanza 1 lyrics written by Anna Bartlett Warner

Requests for information should be addressed to:
Zonderkidz, *Grand Rapids, Michigan* 49530

Library of Congress Cataloging-in-Publication Data

Jesus loves me / pictures by Hector Borlasca.
    p. cm. -- (I can read! Level 2)
  ISBN 978-0-310-71619-8 (softcover)
1. Jesus Christ--Juvenile literature. 2. Jesus Christ--Songs and music--Juvenile
    literature. 3. Children's songs. I. Borlasca, Hector.
  BT302.J573 2008
  232--dc22

                                                                2007034331

Zonderkidz is a trademark of Zondervan.

Editor: Betsy Flikkema
Art direction & design: Jody Langley

Printed in Hong Kong

09 10 11 12 • 5 4

ZONDERkidz

I Can Read!

1

BEGINNING
READING

Jesus Loves Me

pictures by Hector Borlasca

Jesus loves me! This I know,

for the Bible tells me so.

Little ones to him belong.

They are weak, but he is strong.

7

Yes, Jesus loves me.

Yes, Jesus loves me.

Yes, Jesus loves me.

The Bible tells me so.

Jesus loves me! This I know,

as he loved so long ago.

He takes children on his knee,

saying, "Let them come to me."

Yes, Jesus loves me.

Yes, Jesus loves me.

Yes, Jesus loves me.

The Bible tells me so.

Jesus loves me still today,

walking with me on my way.

As a friend, he likes to give

light and love to all who live.

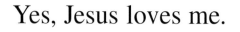

Yes, Jesus loves me.

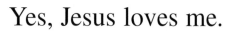

Yes, Jesus loves me.

Yes, Jesus loves me.

The Bible tells me so.

BIBLE

Jesus loves me! He will stay
close beside me all the way.

He has washed away my sin
and lets his little child come in.

Yes, Jesus loves me.

Yes, Jesus loves me.

Yes, Jesus loves me.

The Bible tells me so.

Jesus loved us when he died.

He pushed the gate of heaven wide.

He is watching from above.

Jesus I will always love.

Jesus Loves Me

Je sus loves me! This I know, for the Bi-ble tells me so.

Lit-tle ones to him be long. They are weak but he is strong.

Yes, Je - sus loves me. Yes, Je - sus loves me.

Yes, Je - sus loves me. The Bi - ble tells me so.